1 Buttercup

2 Tiger

3 Macaroni

4 Coco

10 Buster

One Guinea Pig Is Not Enough

5 Pigwiggin

9 Peaches

8 Floradora

7 Plato

6 Tex

One Guinea Pig

Dutton Children's Books

NEW YORK

Is Not Enough

• Kate Duke •

Copyright © 1998 by Kate Duke
Library of Congress Cataloging-in-Publication Data

Duke, Kate.
One Guinea pig is not enough/by Kate Duke.
1st ed.   p. cm.
Summary: A little guinea pig is quite lonely until, one by one,
nine others, plus ten of their moms or dads, add to the general excitement.
ISBN 0-525-45918-9
[1. Guinea pigs—Fiction. 2. Counting.] I. Title.
PZ7.D886On 1998 [E]—dc21 97-21367 CIP AC

Published in the United States 1998 by Dutton Children's Books,
a member of Penguin Putnam Inc.
375 Hudson Street, New York, New York 10014
Designed by Amy Berniker
Printed in Hong Kong   First Edition
1 3 5 7 9 10 8 6 4 2

The artwork was rendered in acrylic, watercolor, pencil,
colored pencil, and colored inks.

To Sidney

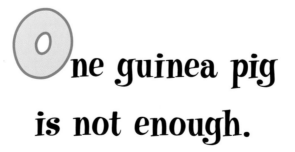ne guinea pig
is not enough.

One guinea pig is a lonely guinea pig.

One lonely guinea pig

plus one other lonely guinea pig

make two

smiling guinea pigs.

1+1=2

Two smiling guinea pigs

plus one silly guinea pig

make three

giggling guinea pigs.

2+1=3

Three giggling guinea pigs

plus one singing guinea pig

make four

dancing guinea pigs.

3+1=4

Four dancing guinea pigs

plus one jumping guinea pig

make five

flying guinea pigs.

4+1=5

Five flying guinea pigs

plus one proud guinea pig

make six

sorry guinea pigs.

Six sorry guinea pigs

plus one smart guinea pig

make seven

helpful guinea pigs.

6+1=7

Seven helpful guinea pigs

plus one hungry guinea pig

make eight

picnicking guinea pigs.

7+1=8

Eight picnicking guinea pigs

plus one sneaky guinea pig

make nine

fighting guinea pigs.

8+1=9

Nine fighting guinea pigs

plus one big guinea pig

make ten

good guinea pigs.

9+1=10

Ten good guinea pigs

plus ten mom or dad guinea pigs

make twenty

hugging guinea pigs—

10+10=20

and twenty is plenty.